Beatrice and the Basilisk

By

Bruce McCandless III

Beatrice and the Basilisk

By Bruce McCandless III
Copyright 2013 Ninth Planet Press, Inc.
Austin, Texas

This is a work of fiction.
No resemblance to any person or place, real
or imagined, is either intended or endorsed.

An early version of this story appeared in *The Mythic Circle*.

For Emma and Carson

ISBN: 0615609015
ISBN 13: 9780615609010

basilisk: (n) a large, usually winged reptile; a dragon.

Beatrice: (pn) a knobby-kneed 12-year-old girl; a middle-schooler.

Beatrice and the Basilisk

CHAPTER ONE

The dragon was headed straight for Beatrice McIlvaine's house, which was bad enough. Beatrice was sound asleep. This didn't help. But what really made the outlook bleak for everyone concerned was the nature of this particular dragon. Its teeth were as sharp as shredded steel. Its eyes were the color of blood in deep veins. The creature's tail, though short, was barbed, and could batter down the stoutest door. No bright blade had ever punctured this black hide, or gashed this baleful head.

Beatrice woke up. It was three o'clock in the morning, and her eyes were wet with tears.

Anne McIlvaine heard the squeal of the shower door just after five a.m. This struck her as odd, because her daughter was a girl of precise habits. Beatrice hoisted herself out of bed every morning at 5:30 and headed for the shower. After she dried off, she padded into the kitchen, put the water on for Anne's instant coffee, and tried not to watch until it boiled. Then she walked back up the hallway and tapped on her mother's door. Anne McIlvaine was a sound sleeper. Sometimes Beatrice had to come in and give her a shake. Two shakes, actually.

Mornings were hectic in the McIlvaine house. Anne had to be out the door by six to make it to work at the Flying D Stables in time. There she had fourteen horses to feed and turn out, fourteen stalls to clean and sand and level. Some of the horses needed medicine or a change of dressing. A few needed extra hay, or a vitamin tablet, or, increasingly these days, a *multi-vitamin supplement powder with probiotic.* All of them, Anne figured, needed a kind word and a pat on the neck. She worked until mid-morning at the stables, and after this she helped out at the feed store just across the highway. In the afternoon she went back to the Flying D to bring the horses in from pasture. The little girls from the new subdivisions out on the lake showed up after school for their riding lessons, and assorted doctors and accountants stopped by to say hello to their Rustys and Sparkles and John Henrys. After they left, Anne fed and watered and settled the horses for the evening. On a good night, she was home by six-thirty.

It was a grueling schedule. Sometimes her back ached from hauling hay, or her leg went black and blue where the new colt had kicked her. But even working twelve-hour days, Anne McIlvaine barely made enough money to pay the rent and the bills and to keep her family in groceries. She wouldn't have been able to do it without the help of her daughter.

Beatrice was an odd, intense little girl. Anne didn't pretend to understand her. She was always doing something, always in motion, studying her Texas History or Earth Science for school, dribbling her basketball left-handed in the driveway or tackling the endless small chores around the house. Chubby and mostly bald as a baby, Beatrice had become a skinny little girl with a shock of barbarous red hair. She looked younger than her age but acted considerably older. After the death of her father two years ago, it was if Bea had gone from ten years old to twenty-eight with only a single day in between. She did most of the cooking and cleaning now, and she kept a sharp eye on little Frank when he got home from school. And she did all of this without complaint, seemingly without a second thought.

In fact she was far more mature than her mother, Anne reflected—who ought to be out of bed by now. Anne sat up with a start and looked at the clock. It was only 5:19. Still early. But maybe since she was awake, she'd surprise her daughter and start breakfast herself. Beatrice wasn't used to being out-earlied. This was going to be fun. Anne swung her feet out from under the blankets and cinched her flannel robe around her waist. She padded down the hallway past the bathroom. In the kitchen, the water for her instant coffee was already boiling. Beatrice was leaning over the sink to look out the window. Her wet hair hung lank to her shoulders. She held a spatula in her left hand, and she was staring up at the sky.

CHAPTER TWO

The school bus was late this morning. Beatrice dug a pencil out of her book bag and tried to check her math homework while she waited. It was fractions again: multiplication of fractions, division of fractions, fractions till her eyes went funny and she imagined how nice it would be just to give that old oven a good cleaning tonight. After she'd made dinner, of course. And vacuumed the rug. And, yes, finished her homework—which was getting harder and harder to do. Especially with the dreams she was having lately: the dreams of some ancient evil riding the night sky, a speck of malice, distant still but getting closer.

She was checking number nine again when she smelled crème rinse and bubble gum. She knew it was Jennifer Ramos without lifting her eyes from the page.

"Beatrice, I can't believe you!"

"What?" said Beatrice. "What'd I do?"

"I thought we were wearing dresses today."

Jen was a little paranoid sometimes. Like every morning before school. Jennifer Ramos hated the little neighborhood of duplexes and convenience stores where she and Beatrice lived. *No magic*, she often said. *No style*. She was determined to glam it up. Today she sported jeggings under a maroon knit dress and her mother's leather coat. Her jet-black hair gleamed, and she was wearing lip gloss and a new pair of black Australian suede boots.

"Ugh," said Beatrice. She slapped her own forehead. "You're right. I'm sorry. I completely forgot."

"You never forget things, Bea. Oh my God. This is a *joke*. I bet Allison and Ginny are wearing jeans today too, right? And I'm gonna look like a geek? I texted you right when I got up."

"I forgot to charge my phone. Things have been crazy lately."

"I've got a bad feeling about this."

"I forgot, okay? You look really cute. I was thinking about something else, and…" Beatrice's eyes left Jen to focus on her little brother, who was emerging from a wooded lot twenty-five yards down the street. "Oh, Lord. Frank's gonna be late for school again. FRANKIE!"

Franklin McIlvaine froze in his tracks, surprised and embarrassed that his sister had caught him playing hooky. He was small for a nine-year-old. He had pale reddish hair and freckles like Beatrice's, but brown eyes instead of green. Truth was, he hadn't planned on going to school today at all. He cradled an electronic metal detector in one arm, his fourth grade reading workbook in the other. His earmuffs were looped around his neck. He wore them when he was working, combing the earth for the treasure Jean Lafitte had reportedly buried in the area two centuries earlier. The earmuffs helped him concentrate. They shut out the world. This morning he had hoped to run a thorough scan of the weedy banks of the old gravel pit, an area where his father had once discovered three spoons, a bent screwdriver, and a perfectly good pocket knife, all of which he gave to Frank.

He could forget those plans now. He had emerged from his hiding place just a few minutes too soon. Beatrice was sure to call from the junior high to check on him at some point during the day. Frank knew that if the elementary school secretary said he wasn't there, he'd face a grounding even worse than the last one, when he hadn't been allowed out of the house even to go to the mailbox.

Without a word, Frank McIlvaine turned and trudged in the opposite direction, back toward Ed White Elementary. He wasn't happy about it. He'd never find a single doubloon at this rate. His family would be stuck in the ratty duplex on Bellgrove forever. *Chalk up another one for St. Beatrice,* he thought aloud.

He kicked every rock he could find.

CHAPTER THREE

"GOOD MORNING, STUDENTS! I'm Mrs. Knowles, and I'll be your teacher while Miss Cabaza is out with what appears to be a bout of Spanish influenza. There's a high pressure area stationary over much of the Gulf Coast, which means we'll have splendid conditions for mathematics for the rest of this week—and possibly next week as well. I trust you've all completed your homework."

Beatrice decided Mrs. Knowles looked like the kind of woman who stayed home and baked things filled with raisins. She was a big, bulgy potato sack of a woman, with cookie-dough arms and pudgy fingers. Her hair was honey blonde, probably dyed, and her green eyes crinkled to slits when she laughed, which was often.

Bea's class groaned at the mention of homework. Usually when they had a substitute teacher, homework went uncollected. Unmentioned. Politely ignored. Everyone knew subs were basically clueless. As if to illustrate the point, this one had turned her back to the class. As she wrote her name in loopy letters on the chalkboard, Antonio Blackledge prepared to welcome Mrs. Innocencia Knowles to Seabrook Intermediate School. Beatrice watched the boy stuff a mushy spit wad into the hollow cylinder of a ball point pen, then raise the cylinder to his lips.

"Now, Antonio," said Mrs. Knowles, though she was still facing the board, "do you really want to do that? It's a slippery slope, my friend. First it's spit wads. Next you shoplift a few Kit Kats. Pretty soon you've got a hot Xbox on your hands—which will buy you a felony rap in this state, by the way—and you're looking at hard time. How long do you think it's going to be before you find yourself lying face down on the floor of a service station, staring at the motor oil additives on the bottom shelf as a strapping young police officer reads you your rights? Hmm?"

Antonio slowly lowered the cylinder. His mouth made a few tentative shapes, as if it was trying to come up with words without the help of his brain. His eyes were the size of walnuts.

Mrs. Knowles worked the first three homework problems on the board. All three of her answers were incorrect.

❦

The substitute glanced up from her desk. "I suppose you're wondering why I asked you to stay after class," she said.

"Did I do something wrong?" asked Beatrice.

"Heavens, no," said Mrs. Knowles. "I just wanted you to know that we're aware of your predicament."

"Predicament?" Beatrice figured she'd be able to handle fractions eventually. It wasn't really a "predicament" at this point. It was more of a "nuisance." "What, with Math?"

"I admit my ciphering is a little rusty. Got too used to the abacus, I suppose. Leaning on technology.

Always a mistake. What I mean..." Mrs. Knowles dropped her voice to a whisper. "What I mean is, the predicament with the *basilisk*."

Beatrice was silent. She glanced around the empty room.

"You're kind of freaking me out here, Mrs. Knowles."

"I get that a lot. But listen. It's going to be here *tonight*, child. Are you prepared?"

"You mean the dragon?" said Beatrice. "It's real? I wasn't—?"

"Dreaming? No. But you're in luck. And you may ask me for any three things you desire."

"Why?"

"It's not a question of why, child. It's a question of *when*."

Beatrice thought for only a moment.

"A sword," she said.

"Against this monster? *Ach*. Might as well ask for a soup spoon. Have you considered a MANPAD?"

Beatrice frowned. "I'm not sure what..."

"Man-Portable Air Defense System. You know. The Stinger missile. It's a Raytheon product, I believe."

The portly substitute went to the board. With a piece of blue chalk in her left hand she sketched what could have been a surface-to-air missile. Or possibly a tapeworm. It didn't work. Bea's mind was made up.

"Not just any sword, Mrs. Knowles."

"No?"

Beatrice looked down at her books. She'd read once of a weapon so powerfully enchanted that it made the warrior who held it invincible; a blade so bright that the first time it was drawn in battle, it blinded seventeen of its bearer's enemies.

"Excalibur," she said.

The big woman snapped the chalk she was holding. A faint smile played on her face, as if she could see the fabled weapon in her head.

"Not just any sword is right," said the woman. "That thing is bigger than you are."

"Excalibur," Beatrice repeated.

Mrs. Knowles held Beatrice's gaze for almost a minute. Finally, almost imperceptibly, she nodded. "Don't forget your homework," she added.

CHAPTER FOUR

The dragon had been flying for five nights.

It wasn't just any dragon. Technically, it was a winged basilisk of the sub-species *draco horribilis,* first described by Asclepius in his pioneering *Natural Studies* in 456 B.C. Asclepius called the creature by another name as well, a title he translated as best he could from the long-dead Eastern language that gave it birth. This name was "Heart Eater." The translation was a good try, but it lacked nuance. In the original tongue, "heart" actually meant something closer to *spirit,* or *soul.*

The soul eater lived on an island deep in the southern seas, where red fruit rotted on sagging branches and night drew a curtain of bats across the sky. The rusted frame of an old prop-driven airplane—a Lockheed Electra 10E, from the looks of it—lay like a broken crucifix in the forest on the island's north side. Wild pigs populated the west and south. Mostly they foraged for food in the low-lying grasslands. Visitors occasionally wondered if there had been a larger population of pigs in the past. They wondered because of the bones. Great piles of them whitened in the tropical sun. But not all of them belonged to pigs. Some of them were clearly human.

Now, far from those restless seas, moonlight flooded the Texas coastal prairie. Scraps of cloud hurried across the heavens like deserters from a desperate army. The dragon had been flying five nights, but it wasn't tired. It fed on flocks of migratory songbirds. It sucked clouds from the air to slake its thirst. It circled twice. It pulled in its long wings, and began its descent.

Beatrice gripped the slats of her headboard and realized she wasn't breathing. Then she saw it again. A moving shadow severed the shafts of moonlight in her room. She took a deep breath and slid out of bed. In the silvery light, she saw Alexander the Great watching her with drowsy eyes.

"Shhhhh," she cautioned the cat.

The sword stood like a buttress in a corner of her bedroom. It was heavy in her hands. *Too heavy?* she wondered. Beatrice slipped off the velvet scabbard. The great blade glowed a shade somewhere between blue and white. It made a faint humming sound, as if it had been struck by a hammer.

Alexander's eyes opened wide.

In the hallway, Beatrice closed Frank's door. She padded into her mother's bedroom and kissed Anne McIlvaine softly on the cheek. Then she tiptoed through the kitchen to the back door.

"Alexander," she said, nudging him away with her foot. "No. Stay back."

Holding the sword in both hands, Beatrice stepped out into the night.

CHAPTER FIVE

Mrs. Knowles wasn't in Math the next morning. Miss Cabaza was back, as fit as a fireman, and she wasn't at all pleased when Beatrice, ordinarily one of her best students, came up with the wrong answer for problem number six on page 189. Beatrice felt lucky to have found page 189 to begin with. She scarcely knew what she was doing. Her knees still trembled when she thought of what had happened only a few hours earlier. She knew she had to find Mrs. Knowles. It was quite literally a matter of life and death.

Mrs. Knowles, it turned out, was in the gym.

She wore the same royal blue crepe dress as yesterday, but it was accented now with high-top basketball sneakers and a steel whistle on a yellow lanyard. She looked about as much like a gym teacher, Beatrice concluded, as Jennifer Ramos looked like a linebacker.

"GOOD MORNING, GIRLS!" she announced. Beatrice realized Mrs. Knowles's voice was exactly the same shape as her body. "I'm sorry to report that Mrs. Grant has developed rather a nasty case of laryngitis. Or that's the assumption, anyway, because no one in the front office quite understood what the poor dear was trying to say when she called in sick this morning. At any rate, since I have been advised that my pedagogical talents are not perfectly suited to the pursuit of mathematics, my assignment today is, as you may have guessed, P.E. Now how many of you here have sailed around the Cape of Good Hope on a three-masted schooner? No one? Well, I can't say I blame you. It can be a dreadful voyage, especially if you're transporting goats. But if you'd ever made the trip, you might understand the practical benefits of excelling in our program for today, which is ROPE CLIMBING."

Jennifer Ramos was wearing blue Lycra tights and a Rice University sweatshirt. She rolled her eyes.

"Who is this psycho?" she whispered. "Mrs. Grunt never makes us climb the rope. I thought we were gonna do *zumba* again. I don't know *how* to climb rope."

"I can't even climb out of bed," said the girl beside her.

Beatrice narrowed her eyes as she traced the length of the stout hawser. "How high do you think that is?" she said.

Beatrice came closest to reaching the top. She was twenty-eight feet up, only a body-length from the ceiling, when she had to stop.

"Come on, Bea!" yelled Jen. "You're almost there!"

Jen generally ignored anything that happened in P.E. In her opinion, P.E. was where fashion went to die. But even *she* was excited by her best friend's effort. Bea wasn't the strongest girl in class, or the fastest. But she was typically the most determined, and everyone knew to stay out of her way when she got that Beatrice look in her eyes: the one where she squinted a lot, and her lips went thin and colorless.

"You're stuck?" said Mrs. Knowles. "You need help?"

"I can do it." Beatrice looked at the ceiling, then down at her teacher. "It was scared of the sword," she said. "I raised it up and the sword made a sound like it was singing and it frightened the dra—*frightened* it."

Mrs. Knowles shrugged. "It'll be back."

"I know," said Beatrice. From her vantage point high on the rope, she gazed around the gymnasium like the look-out on one of the pirate ships Frank was always reading about. Below her, the girls in her class sat in a circle on the mats at the base of the rope. Their faces were turned upward toward her. Jen was clearly confused by what she was hearing.

The boys were playing dodge ball on the other side of the gym. The grainy red balls flew back and forth like bullets, and boys in white t-shirts and green shorts charged and fell back, screaming at each other over the center line. Little Larry Micholajek, a scarecrow of a kid, all elbows and earlobes, had tripped while going for a ball. Now he lay on the wood floor, groping for his glasses. He couldn't see Antonio Blackledge, who had scooped up the same ball as it rolled across the center line and was laughing like a hyena as he closed in on Larry.

Antonio heaved the ball just as Mrs. Knowles's steel whistle sounded. The noise was like a hundred tea kettles come to a boil. Antonio turned instantly to locate the source of sound and when he did, the dodge ball ricocheted off Larry Micholajek's hip. Oddly, the ball seemed to accelerate before it struck Antonio squarely on the side of the head. He went down like a cartoon thug, stunned but not hurt.

Mrs. Knowles's voice cut through the shrieks and echoes of the gym.

"Remember, Antonio!" she fog-horned. "You have the right to remain SILENT! You have the right to an attorney! If you cannot AFFORD an attorney, one—"

"Mrs. Knowles?" said Beatrice.

The big woman refocused her attention on the rope. "Yes, dear?"

"I think it's coming back."

"I shouldn't doubt it."

"*Tonight*, I mean."

"Have you told your mother?"

Beatrice shook her head. "My mom doesn't need to know. She's under a lot of pressure at work."

"Your brother?"

"Head case. Very fragile."

"I know the type. Likes to eat bugs?"

"Not that type. I need a horse."

"A horse? I'm still liking the surface-to-air missile idea. Have you—?"

"Not just any horse," Beatrice stated. She set her mouth hard.

"I might have guessed. The whole Joan of Arc thing, right? Which horse did you have in mind? Secretariat? Bucephalus?"

"A different one."

"How different?"

"Pegasus."

Mrs. Knowles bowed her head. Pegasus was the winged horse of the Muses, a creature born of blood and mist and the troubled dreams of a dozen demi-gods. He was as swift as a shooting star, as sullen and deadly as a summer typhoon.

"I hope you know what you're doing," said the substitute.

Beatrice summoned her last ounce of strength and pulled herself up the rope again. Her right hand was inches away from the paneled ceiling when she lost her grip with her left. She slid thirty feet to the mat and landed hard on her back. Her classmates crowded around her. Jen offered her hand, but Beatrice waved it off.

"I'm all right," Beatrice insisted, once she was able to catch her breath. "I'm fine."

CHAPTER SIX

Beatrice's father was the sort of fireman who had trouble resisting an opportunity to further the cause of public safety. Pat McIlvaine was on a fishing trip with his daughter one blustery Sunday morning in March when he spotted a dog-sized piece of tire tread sitting in the roadway fifty yards ahead of their car. Two thirds of the way across the Galveston Bridge, Pat McIlvaine stopped his battered Suburban, opened the driver's side door, and jogged over to drag the rubber tread out of the road. Beatrice had been told to stay put. Just as her father turned to head back to the car, a sheet of corrugated plastic roofing material slid out of the bed of a passing pickup. The sheet hit the road and pinwheeled at sixty miles an hour toward Pat McIlvaine. Beatrice watched as it knocked her father down. It wasn't until she'd run to him that she found it had also punctured Pat McIlvaine's throat. There are ten pints of blood in the human body. Few wounds are as effective at draining them as a gash in the carotid artery, largest of the vessels that speed oxygenated blood from the heart to the brain. Pat McIlvaine died quickly. One can imagine. Or maybe not. On the few occasions when Beatrice allowed herself to look back at that day, what she remembered most was the pain in her own throat. She'd screamed so hard that she couldn't talk for three days.

And once she *could* talk, she didn't want to. She'd watched her father die by the side of a road. Was there really anything else to say?

CHAPTER SEVEN

Beatrice wrapped three potatoes in aluminum foil and placed them in the oven. She was proud of her ability to reuse foil. This was the fourth round of potatoes she'd baked in the same stained silvery wrappers. She dropped a slab of frozen peas in the saucepan, added half a cup of water, and turned the burner on low. She scrambled eggs in a plastic bowl and mixed up a pitcher of orange juice. Wednesday night dinner—also known as "Friday night dinner," "Monday night dinner," and "Tuesday night dinner"—coming up.

Prep time: Minimal.

Nutritional value: High.

Wow factor: Zero.

Possibly *less* than zero.

Frank showed up at the back door twenty minutes after she'd called him. He carried the metal detector over his shoulder like a rifle, but his earmuffs were still in place.

"Sorry, Frankie. Dinner won't be for another half-hour. Mom called and said she has a sick horse."

"What?" said Frank.

"Dinner!" said Beatrice. She pointed to his ears, and Frank finally got the picture. He took off the ear-muffs. "We'll eat in half an hour."

"I can cover a lot of ground by then. I'm going back out."

"Did you do your geography homework yet?"

"I told you, I don't know where it is."

"You don't know where *anything* is, which is exactly why you'd better get back into that pigsty of yours and do your geography. I've been doing home-work all afternoon while you were out there picking up rusty nails."

Frank flopped onto the couch and started thumb-ing through the Sharper Image catalogue.

"Believe me," he grumbled. "When I find treasure, I'm not going to eat stupid scrambled eggs anymore. We didn't eat eggs for dinner when Dad was around."

Beatrice counted to ten, trying to control her temper.

"Well, now we do, okay? And I'm going to make them like I always do, and you're going to eat them because you're nine years old and your arms look like toothpicks."

This was true. Frank wore long-sleeve shirts even in the summer so no one would see how skinny his arms were. But he didn't like to be reminded of the fact. The catalogue went flying. Frank stormed out of the room. Beatrice speared frozen peas with a fork.

Frankie was a troubled kid. Once, after their father died, he'd slept for twenty-six hours straight. Searching for buried treasure was the first thing he'd managed to work up any enthusiasm for, and Beatrice hesitated to distract him from it. Evidently she had, though. She could hear her brother throwing shoes against the walls of his room. Maybe it was her lot in life to have Frankie hate her, Beatrice reflected. Maybe they would never be friends, like normal brothers and sisters. But if that was the case, so be it. She was going to keep the family together if it killed her.

Alexander the Great leapt from the table to the counter-top and landed with an undignified grunt. Beatrice had to laugh at his pitiful expression.

"You're not hungry," she scolded. "I already gave you your dinner."

Alexander licked his lips and blinked solemnly at her. *I'm surrounded by misfits*, thought Beatrice. Her father had only agreed to adopt the cat after it loitered at the back door for three weeks. No one ever found out that Beatrice had been setting out tuna fish for the animal every afternoon when she got home from school. Her father named him Alexander the Great because he figured the cat had, like the human Alexander, probably conquered all of his own known world. Alexander soon proved himself to be a scoundrel and a blackguard, a street fighter capable of routing even an eighty-pound Weimaraner who wandered up the driveway looking for a little excitement. Now, though, the cat was getting old. There were fine white hairs interspersed with the black on his head and chest. One of his ears was split in two, and there was a large gray scar shaped like a parenthesis between his eyes. He had a habit of collapsing whenever and wherever he felt sleepy. At the moment, this was the peeling, coffee-stained counter-top. The cat watched as Beatrice stirred milk into the eggs. His eyes were half-closed. They only opened again when she tossed him a triangle of cheese.

Just then she heard a metallic crash outside the house.

Probably raccoons getting into the garbage, Beatrice told herself. Sure, that was it. *Raccoons.* She was fine. She picked the fork up off the floor. She held her hand over her chest as if she could catch her frantic heart.

It was two a.m. when she woke up this time.

Alexander raced her to the back door, his black tail twitching with excitement and irritation. She had trouble keeping him inside.

The moon was nearly full. The clouds were dark with bright edges, like a photographic negative, and the scrubby field behind the house seemed to glow. Pegasus thundered toward her like a dream, his hooves a mounting drum beat. The animal pulled up just short of where she stood. He pawed at the frozen earth, and his breath made steam in the chilly air.

Beatrice clutched her sword with one hand. She climbed up on her mother's mulch box, grabbed the horse's thick mane, and pulled herself onto his back. When the shadow of the dragon passed in front of the moon, Pegasus snorted, as if he was blowing an unpleasant odor out of his lungs. Then he raised his white head, and his cry split the night like a knife through a cotton sheet. The horse's wings welcomed the wind. Soon high clouds dampened Beatrice's hair. Starlight danced in flecks of silver on her arms. The dragon gave chase, but to no avail. The dark thing faded to a speck on the horizon, like a distant dream. Beatrice wore the night like a cloak, and Pegasus made the long miles disappear.

CHAPTER EIGHT

The next day Mrs. Knowles stood behind the lunch room counter, serving up fried fish sandwiches and tater tots. She wore plastic gloves on her hands and a net over her honey-blonde hair.

"Thank goodness you're here, child," she said when she saw Beatrice. "I wasn't sure you would make it."

"I wasn't either," Beatrice admitted.

"You look dreadful. Have you slept? Or eaten?"

"I usually just have a fudgesicle."

"Not today. You'll eat a full meal. Tell me what happened."

"We…I don't know. We like, lured it away. Pegasus was faster. The dragon couldn't keep up. We flew to where there were mountains, and snow, and the trees looked like skeletons sticking up through the ice."

Mrs. Knowles handed a fishwich platter to the boy in line behind Beatrice. Antonio Blackledge thanked her politely before he stepped around Beatrice to get to the ice cream freezer. He'd had his homework ready for Miss Cabaza this morning, and it was entirely possible that Antonio Blackledge had bathed at some point during the last twenty-four hours.

"It won't fall for the same trick twice," said Mrs. Knowles, eyeing Antonio suspiciously. "If you run, it won't chase you. It'll just wait. Basilisks are as patient as glaciers. But not quite as charitable."

"I was afraid of that. It's not going to go away, is it?"

Mrs. Knowles shook her head.

"Tonight, then," said Beatrice.

"What else will you need?"

"Courage, I guess."

"Child, if you had any more guts you wouldn't fit in your clothes. You have faith and a fine, true heart. But you need something more."

"What, then?"

Mrs. Knowles nibbled a tater tot.

"Mrs. Knowles?" said Beatrice.

"Hmm?"

"What do I need?"

"That I can't tell you," said Mrs. Knowles, as she tossed the crusty potato cylinder over one shoulder. "But you'll know. At some point you'll surely know. And when you do, *ask*. Ask as loudly as you can."

"But what…?"

"What, dear?"

"What if I don't know until it's too late?"

Mrs. Knowles frowned, but was silent. Beatrice slid her plate along the serving line. She sat down at her usual table, the one nearest the stage, and ate without tasting her food. Twice Jennifer Ramos asked her what was wrong. Beatrice only shrugged. Just before lunch was over, she scribbled out a set of questions on a paper napkin and went back to the serving line.

Mrs. Knowles was gone.

The Hispanic lady who'd taken her place spoke only a little English. She didn't seem to have any idea who Beatrice was talking about.

"Fudgesicle?" she said.

CHAPTER NINE

Her mother had another colicky mare at the stables that evening, so Beatrice ate dinner alone. She hated to admit it, but her little brother was right. Scrambled eggs with peas was getting old. Frankie was in his bedroom, drinking decaf coffee and watching an old Errol Flynn movie on TV while he recharged the batteries of the metal detector. Frankie was a keen student of pirate behavior. He knew just when to hoist the Blue Peter and how to make an English prelate walk the plank. He could, and frequently would, explain the correct way to raise a gallon jug of brown rum to his parched, blistered lips (index finger through the jug handle; jug itself lifted by the outside angle of the elbow; quaff with a sideways lifting of the head—less exposure of the throat this way). He was definitely the oddest kid she had ever encountered.

Anne McIlvaine arrived home just after ten. The first thing she asked was, "Where's Alexander the Great?" Beatrice was washing dishes. She said she thought the cat was probably hiding from her, just like Frankie was. When Anne took a closer look at her daughter, her heart sank. Beatrice was obviously exhausted. Her red hair was tangled and needed a trim. Her eyes were inflamed, as if she'd been crying.

"Beatrice, what's wrong?"

"What."

Anne put a hand on her daughter's forehead. "You're upset."

"I'm fine."

"Darling, please. Tell me what's wrong."

Beatrice dropped the scrub brush and ran from the sink. Anne knew better than to go after her. She found Frank instead. He was going over his maps.

"Nothing, Mom," he said. "I swear. I even said I'd do the dishes, but she wouldn't let me. She's having another one of her St. Beatrice spasms. She won't let anyone do anything."

"She's tired, Frankie. I'm letting her do too much. She's just..." Anne had to pause for a moment. She bent her head. When she lifted it, she tried to smile. "You find any treasure today?"

Frank frowned.

"Nothing. I never find nothing, Mom."

"Anything, dear. I never find *anything.*"

"Yeah," he said. "That too."

Anne stopped in front of Beatrice's door. She held up one palm, as if she could feel her daughter through the cheap wood panels. She put her cheek and temple against the frame. *Should she try to talk to her daughter? Find out what the problem was?* She sighed once and rubbed her eyes. It was no use. Beatrice never even admitted to *having* problems, which made it difficult to discuss what they were. Anne knew that if she started asking her daughter questions, Beatrice would frown, shake her hair out of her eyes, and offer to make her mother a piece of cinnamon toast. Maybe it was best, Anne thought, to leave her alone for now. Besides, they all needed sleep. It was almost time to get up again.

CHAPTER TEN

nother night.

A shadow.

Beatrice knew this would be their final confrontation. She was going to *make it* the final confrontation. She couldn't go on like this. She was so tired she had trouble remembering her name. Her eyes burned, and at school she felt herself shivering as she tried to keep her head off the desk. Tonight would end it. Either she'd drive the creature out of her head, and out of the clouds, or she'd go spiraling painfully into some forever-sleep and never have to worry about it again.

So they hunted. Together the girl and the winged horse coursed the frigid South Texas sky. They soared over the fire-spitting refineries of Baytown and the giant tankers that inched up the Ship Channel like metal snails on a glistening sidewalk. They circled out over the Gulf of Mexico and back above the scrubby pelican kingdoms of Anahuac and Trinity Bay. The dragon was nowhere to be seen. At last, exhausted and uncertain, with nowhere else to look, Beatrice and Pegasus banked low over Seabrook again, checking to make sure no harm had come to Beatrice's house. Sure enough, it was safe. Beatrice started to wonder if maybe the monster had returned to whatever foul place it had come from.

That's when it hit them.

The basilisk dropped from the canopy of stars like a nightmare turned to lead. Pegasus lunged to his left to avoid the impact, but neither the horse nor Beatrice completely escaped the monster's talons. Beatrice lost her grip on Excalibur. She fell 20 feet and landed on something cold and very hard. She found herself lying face-down in the scrubby field behind her house. She knew Pegasus was hurt too, but she couldn't see him now, so she couldn't be sure how bad the wound was.

The basilisk climbed back up into the night, still silent, visible only as a black smudge against the heavens. The moon was as cool as marble. The stars stood still as they watched.

Beatrice bled from her nose and left ear. Stunned, she propped herself up on one elbow, wiped at her face with the sleeve of her hoodie. Finally, in her pain and fear, she realized what she needed. But she didn't know how to ask for it.

The dragon was a distant kite, barely visible in the pre-dawn sky.

Maybe she could still walk. *If only I can find Pegasus,* she thought. She pulled herself up off the grass. *Then we...* Her left ankle gave way and she hit the ground again. The pain of her injuries was working like a drug inside her, slowing her senses, dulling her thoughts. She knew she had to get up. She knew she had to keep moving.

Now the dragon turned in its long arc, veering around toward her. Beatrice sensed it rather than saw it. *The Heart Eater. Night Thing.* A creature of wordless hatred and infinite malice. The dragon was coming back.

"I'm hurt," she said aloud. "Please."

How long did she have? Two minutes? Three? She couldn't do it herself. What she needed was help. And Mrs. Knowles had said—what had she said?

To ask.

"Somebody, please… Mother! Mom! FRANKIE!"

Beatrice screamed. She screamed till she thought she would rip her own lungs. Nothing. No one could hear her. Where was the creature? She couldn't see it, but she knew it was coming. Suddenly she remembered her phone. She dug it out of her pocket and punched up her mother's number. One ring. Two. Beatrice prayed her mom's cell phone was somewhere near the bed. Anne McIlvaine was fully capable of sleeping through a ringing phone. Anne McIlvaine was fully capable of sleeping through a refinery explosion, when you got right down to it.

Three rings.

There. The shadow.

Four rings. This wasn't going to work.

"Hello?"

"Mom, I'm in the field behind the house. I'm hurt."

"Beatrice? What—?"

"Mom, please. Come outside! I need help!"

It was only a few moments before the back porch light came on at Beatrice's house and Anne McIlvaine appeared at the door. A second later, Frank squeezed past her. He held his metal detector, and his earmuffs were looped around his neck. He peered out into the darkness. He could hear his sister calling, but he couldn't figure out where she was. Or what in the world was happening.

"Frankie!" cried Beatrice. "My SWORD! It's in the drainage ditch. Try to find my sword!"

"Mom?" said Frank.

"Go," said his mother.

"Yeah, but what kind of a sword? A cutlass? A rapier?" In future years it would be said of J. Franklin McIlvaine, a prominent petroleum geologist, that he never met a problem he couldn't make more complicated with a series of well-meaning questions.

His mother was in no mood for conversation. "Anything long and sharp, Frankie. Now *go!*"

Anne turned off the porch light. In the moonlight, finally, she could see where her daughter lay in the field. She saw something else as well. Something awful: a figure in the sky like some giant night bird, distant but growing steadily larger. She clamped her hand over her mouth.

Alexander the Great was already moving. He covered the tiny backyard in a flash. He vaulted up on the woodpile and cleared the chain link fence by a foot.

Beatrice flexed her throbbing ankle. It bent. *Not broken, at least.* She pulled herself up and began limping toward the stand of slender tallow trees.

The basilisk landed just a few yards away from its injured prey. The skin of its wings billowed like the sails of a rotting ship, and its breath was a stench of death and decay. The dragon watched with unblinking red eyes as Beatrice stood and stumbled another few feet.

No need to rush.

The end was near.

One more step and the girl fell again. The dragon flapped its big wings just once and half leaped, half flew to where its quarry lay. It let out a screech of hunger and triumph. The creature's tongue flicked out like a pitchfork as it bent toward Beatrice, saliva dripping from its wicked jaws.

Alexander the Great, son of Philip of Macedon, Prince of All Nations, attacked his enemies where they were strongest. He drove them from the field through boldness and wild force of will. Now the cat that was his namesake sprang, snarling, at the lowered head of Beatrice's tormentor. The dragon didn't see the black blur until just before impact. It wailed with surprise. It dropped to its knees, rolled, whipped its head back and forth on its snakelike neck.

Beatrice crawled toward the trees. She saw Pegasus standing fifty yards away. Blood flowed from his forehead, and he reared in fright and confusion.

Beatrice shouted, "Mom! The HORSE! I need the horse!"

Anne McIlvaine ripped her jacket away from where it had snagged on the fence, and set out across the field.

The dragon's cry was different this time. This time it held anguish. Blood welled in one of the creature's slitted eyes. The basilisk staggered sideways, reeling with pain, as Alexander picked himself up off the ground. The cat's snarl came from deep in his chest. It rose to a shriek when the monster turned toward him.

Alexander was attacking again when he died.

Anne McIlvaine approached the frightened horse slowly. Pegasus had advanced out onto the field toward Beatrice, but he'd stopped before he reached the tallow trees. Anne could see why. Part of the horse's mane was stuck to a long red wound on his forehead. The thick hair covered his left eye, and the partial blindness had panicked him.

Anne held out a handful of the sugar cubes she carried in her jacket pocket. She spoke as softly as she could, given that her heart was pounding like a kettle drum. The big horse backed and circled her, trying to keep her to his right. Finally she reached him. He nudged the sugar cubes out of her hand, and she realized he understood what she was trying to do. Carefully she plucked the lock of hair out of the bloody wound. Pegasus could see again. Before Anne could say another word, the horse charged off toward where Beatrice lay in the trees.

Frank found the sword.

It stood half-submerged in the dirty water of the drainage ditch, and he dried it on his shirt before he started toward the field behind the house. He had just climbed out of the ditch when he met his sister. At least he thought it was his sister. She looked pale and fierce, and she was riding a horse that had wings. *Huge wings.* Thirty feet across, by Frankie's reckoning.

"I found it!" he shouted. "I found it just looking!"

"You did," said Beatrice, and she couldn't quite suppress a small smile. "Keep Mom inside. Protect her, Frankie."

He handed her the sword.

"Did you lose anything else?" said Frank. "Anything made of metal?"

"Too early to tell," said his sister, as she wrapped one hand in the horse's mane.

Excalibur wanted to fight before she did. Of all the great weapons in human history—*Dyrnwyn*; *Durendal*; Beowulf's fearsome *Hrunting*—this one remains the most mysterious. Its provenance and composition are unknown. Some say the sword was forged many centuries ago from metals that fell to earth from the sky; others, that it was alloyed with the tears of angels who watched men wander into darkness, and mourned the loss of every soul. Now the great blade was as gray as the granite in an Irish church, but its song—a deep, persistent hum, like the waking anthem of earth itself—quickened the young girl's heart. Pegasus galloped black mountains of air. Beatrice felt the horse's rage in the pull of his muscled shoulders, in each powerful sweep of his pearl-blue wings.

The enemies stalked each other through corridors of wind and moonlight. Beatrice and the horse were surprised a half-dozen times by the dragon's attacks. Wings pulled tight to its sides, the creature made no sound as it dropped itself through the air, all teeth and talons and rigid malice. Horse and girl were cut again and again: face, shoulders, ribs, back. But again and again they climbed, craning to catch a glimpse of that shadow staining the stars. In the last bleak moments before dawn they found the creature gliding unaware below them. It was the chance they'd been waiting for. Pegasus wheeled left and plunged. Beatrice leveled the sword. It was the only thing she knew to do. They hit the dragon high, between its shoulders, with a force that could have shattered stone.

Maybe you can imagine that brief ballet above the clouds. Maybe you can hear the crunch of metal on bone and the panicked hiss of the basilisk. Girl and horse and dragon beheld each other on a field of frost-edged air. Their shared recognition of powers won and lost came all at once. Beatrice raised Excalibur again, but the dragon fell before she could swing it. The first rays of the sun impaled the creature in its descent, and a pillar of orange and red fire flared in the sky like a giant exclamation point. Early commuters in the Houston metropolitan area reported the sight online and in the papers. Several digital images exist. The Department of Homeland Security has so far declined to comment.

Beatrice McIlvaine had no idea how long she lay in the grass. The ground beneath her was cold, but she held it tight so it wouldn't leave. Her mother's hands stroked her neck and forehead. The horse was gone. She'd seen him leave—seen the wings stretch out to summon the wind. It was okay. She'd never wanted to own him. The sword had vanished too, as soon as the fight was over.

Soon she would stand, she told herself. Soon the two of them—*three*, because Frankie was here as well—would walk to the house. They would carry Alexander's body with them, because Alexander was a hero, and heroes are remembered. Then Beatrice would crawl into bed, and rest for a while, and dream quiet dreams where no shadows lived. She would sleep soundly for the first time in weeks.

But for now the ground was enough.

"Bea," said her mother. "Here. Let me..."

There was that word, thought Beatrice. *The one she'd asked for. The one that finally made sense.*

Help.

Beatrice brushed her dirty hair away from her eyes. She smiled at the sight of the empty field. Eventually, she knew, she would hold out her hand.

End

33880062R00039

Made in the USA
San Bernardino, CA
13 May 2016